This book
belongs to

_____

This educational book was created in cooperation with Children's Television Workshop, producers of SESAME STREET. Children do not have to watch the television show to benefit from this book. Workshop revenues from this book will be used to help support CTW educational projects.

ON MY WAY WITH SESAME STREET™

Volume 11

Morning to Night

Featuring Jim Henson's Sesame Street Muppets

Children's Television Workshop/Funk & Wagnalls

Authors

Anna H. Dickson
Linda Hayward
Deborah Kovacs
H. Monster
Jessie Smith
Pat Tornborg

Illustrators

Ellen Appleby
Richard Brown
Tom Cooke
Robert Dennis
Tom Leigh
Joe Mathieu
Kimberly A. McSparran
Carol Nicklaus

0-8343-0085-0   1 2 3 4 5 6 7 8 9 0

A Parents' Guide to
MORNING TO NIGHT

The concept of time is difficult for young children to grasp. Daily routines provide one way children can understand the passage of time by linking it to actual events. A routine helps children feel more secure because they know what to expect: first they get up, then they eat breakfast, then they get dressed, and so on.

In "Big Bird's Busy Day," children will recognize the events of their own busy days: play group, story time and bath time.

"Bert's Breakfast," "I Can Dress Myself," "Lunchtime," and "Things to Do on a Rainy Day" focus on specific routines.

"When Is Saturday?" is a story about anticipation. Children will learn the days of the week while they enjoy this funny story about Grover.

We hope your children will enjoy spending time with their Sesame Street friends from MORNING TO NIGHT.

**The Editors
SESAME STREET BOOKS**

When Is Saturday?

SUNDAY

It was a quiet Sunday and Grover was bored. "There's nothing to do around here," he said. "Nothing exciting ever happens."

"But, Grover," said his mommy. "Something exciting is going to happen. Your Uncle Georgie is coming to visit us on Saturday!"

"Saturday? That is *very* exciting!" said Grover. "I can hardly wait to show him my new bed, and take him to the zoo, and . . ." Grover stopped. "But when *is* Saturday, Mommy?" he asked. "Is tomorrow Saturday?"

"No, Grover," said his mommy. "Saturday is a week away. Today is Sunday. After that come Monday, Tuesday, Wednesday, Thursday, Friday, and *then* Saturday."

"Oh, my!" said Grover. "That is too many days for me to remember. How will I know when it is going to be Saturday?"

Grover's mommy made him a calendar. It showed all the days of the week. She drew a circle around Saturday. "Let's put this calendar on the wall," she said. "We'll cross out each day when it's over. That way you can always see how many days are left until Saturday."

Before going to bed that night Grover crossed out Sunday on his calendar. "Today was Sunday," he said to himself. "Five more days until Saturday."

MONDAY

The next morning Grover looked at his calendar. "Today is Monday," he said. "Monday is housecleaning day." He helped his mother do the cleaning. Then he made a little tent-house, and he cleaned that, too.

On Monday afternoon Grover, Prairie Dawn and Herry Monster made animals out of clay. Herry Monster made a clay kitten. Prairie Dawn made a big clay dragon. Grover made a clay cow.

On Monday night Grover drew another X on his calendar. "Today was Monday," he thought as he went to bed. "Four more days until Saturday."

TUESDAY

On Tuesday Grover went to the store with his mother. They bought lots of vegetables to make a big pot of soup.

That night Grover made another X on his calendar. "Tuesday was vegetable soup day," he said. "Only three more days until Saturday."

WEDNESDAY

On Wednesday Grover went to Ernie and Bert's house to play. They made a building with blocks.

Wednesday afternoon Ernie and Bert and Grover went to the library with Big Bird. It was Story Day. They heard a story called "Rumplestiltskin." Grover loved it.

That night, as Grover made an X on Wednesday, he said, "Wednesday was Story Day. Only two more days until Saturday."

THURSDAY

On Thursday Grover played jump rope with Herry Monster and Cookie Monster. Grover jumped 53 times without missing!

Cookie Monster and Grover went to Grover's house afterwards. Grover's mother let them play with some old clothes. They played dress-up all afternoon.

Grover's mother said, "Why don't you ask Cookie Monster to stay overnight tonight?"

"Oh, Mommy!" said Grover. "What a wonderful idea!"

Just before they went to sleep, Grover made another X on his calendar. "Thursday Cookie came to stay," he said happily. "One more day until Saturday."

FRIDAY

Friday was the day Grover's mommy always took him to the park. Grover played on the slide with Cookie Monster. He pushed Big Bird on the swings. Then Big Bird pushed him.

Then they all went to Grover's house and had cookies and milk.

On Friday night, as Grover made an X on his calendar, he said, "Friday was park day. Tomorrow is Saturday. Oh, my goodness! No more days until Saturday. Uncle Georgie will be here tomorrow. I think I will make up a little poem to surprise him."

SATURDAY

Grover woke up early on Saturday. He looked at his calendar. "Today is the day," he said. "Uncle Georgie is coming."

He hurried into the kitchen for breakfast.

Just as Grover and his mommy were finishing their cereal, the doorbell rang.

It was Uncle Georgie! Grover was so happy to see him!

"Hello, Uncle Georgie!" Grover shouted, giving him a big hug.

"Hello, Grover!" said Uncle Georgie, giving him just as big a hug. "What have you been doing?"

"I have learned something new," said Grover. "And I made up a poem to tell you about it."

"My poem is called 'The Days of the Week.'

"Sunday, Monday,
Do I know another?
Yes, I do! Tuesday!
No need to ask my mother.
Next comes Wednesday,
I am sure of that.
After which comes Thursday,
I will give myself a pat.
The next day is Friday,
I can say the days out loud!
And the last day is Saturday,
Oh, I am so proud."

BERT'S BEST BREAKFASTS

Oatmeal Burgers

To serve one—
What you need:
leftover cooked oatmeal
bread crumbs
½ tablespoon of butter

What you do:
Take a bowl of leftover cooked oatmeal out of the refrigerator. With a large, round spoon, dish out patties about 2 inches wide and about ½ inch thick. Then, with clean hands, put them on a plate covered with bread crumbs. Turn them over once, so that both sides are covered with crumbs. Next, for each oatmeal burger, put ½ tablespoon of butter in a frying pan. Fry the oatmeal burgers until they are dark brown and crispy on both sides. Then put them in a bowl and pour some milk on them, or put a little spoonful of apple butter on each one.

Oatmeal Soup

To serve two—

What you need:
⅓ cup of old-fashioned oats
1½ cups of water
½ cup of milk
¼ teaspoon of salt
¼ cup of raisins

What you do:
Pour the water and milk into a pan on top of the stove, and bring them to a boil. Then stir in the raisins, oats, and salt. Turn down the heat, and let the mixture bubble gently for about 7 minutes. Stir it 3 or 4 times while it's cooking. When it's ready, just pour and eat.

Note: Adult supervision is suggested.

Bert's Breakfast

Can you guess what Bert is cooking?

oatmeal

cups

bowls

glasses

plates

cabinet

cookbooks

can opener

coffeepot

toaster

spice rack

teakettle

funnel

stove

sink

pan

oven

apron

potholders

dishtowel

frying pan

colander

refrigerator

sifter

measuring spoons

measuring cup

pancake turner

spatula

grater

rolling pin

spoon

cutting board

knife

fork

ladle

egg beater

Getting Dressed

sock   saddle shoes

Can you put on your socks?

Can you put on your overalls?

turtleneck

Can you pull on your shirt?

hard hat

scarf

cowgirl hat

zipper

Can you zip up your jacket?

Can you buckle your belt?

top hat

bow tie

nightcap

collar

cape

Can you fasten your boots?

pocket

Can you put on your gloves?

cowboy hat

vest

cuff

Can you button your pajamas?

Can you snap your snaps?

I Can Dress Myself

I can dress myself.

I can button my underwear.

I can snap my shirt.

I can zip up my blue jeans. 	I can buckle my belt. 
I can put on my socks. 	I can pull on my boots. 

I can hook my vest.

I can tie my bandanna.

I can put on my jacket.

I can pin on my badge.

I can put on my hat.

Oh, I am so proud!

I can dress myself.

Prairie Dawn's Room

It is raining today.
Can you guess what Prairie Dawn
is going to wear?

rain hat

spaceship

raincoat

doll

closet

hanger

slacks

dress

blouse

teddy bear

umbrella

party shoes

ball

sneakers

sweate

truck

blue jeans

undershirt

pillow

skirt

underpants

jumper

baseball cap

jacket

lamp

bed

socks

night table

bedspread

dresse

toy chest

rubber boots

toy train

sun hat

rocking chair

toy robot

blocks

baseball bat

Lunchtime

Ernie made a peanut butter sandwich.
Which picture shows what Ernie did first?
Which picture shows what Ernie did last?

Things to Do on a Rainy Day

Susan and Gordon have invited their friends to come over and play. There are lots of things to do indoors on a rainy day.

Bob and the Honkers make music.

Betty Lou reads a book.

Susan and Ernie make macaroni jewelry.

Bert makes a clay pigeon.

Grover makes a card for his mommy.

Big Bird and Gordon
play checkers.

Cookie Monster plays house
under the table.

Home
Sweet
Home

Telly pastes
a collage.

Herry and Prairie Dawn
share blocks.

Big Bird's Busy Day

Good morning, Radar! Time to get up. It's another busy day on Sesame Street.

Let's eat breakfast!

Let's clean up our nest!

We have important things to do at play group.

We like digging.

We like swinging.

We like playing.

Dinnertime!

Bath time!

Story time! Good night, Radar.
Tomorrow is another busy day.
Sleep tight.

I Am a Monster

I am a Monster.
My name is Herry.

I am big.

I am furry.

I am strong.

I live on Sesame Street.
Every day I go walking
in my neighborhood.

This is Big Bird.
He is big, but he
is not a Monster.
He is a bird.

This is Oscar.
He is furry, but is
he a Monster?
I don't know, but
he sure is a Grouch!

Here are Ernie and Bert.
They are not big.
They are not furry.
And they are not Monsters.

Oh.
Here is a Monster.
He is the Cookie Monster.

And here is
another Monster.
He is lovable, furry
old Grover.

Some Monsters eat everything.
Some Monsters like to help.
And some
Monsters look
scary.
But all
Monsters
are brave.

Well, most of
the time they
are brave.

This is a
Monster family
at dinner.

At night when I go to bed, I dream sweet Monster dreams.

WHAT TIME IS IT?

seven o'clock

Good morning, Farley. It's time to get up.

eight o'clock

Oh, boy! Scrambled eggs for breakfast!

eight thirty

Good-bye! Have a nice day at work.

nine o'clock

Good-bye! Have a good day at school.

twelve o'clock

I hope it's spaghetti!

I hope it's peanut butter!

one o'clock

two o'clock

three thirty

six o'clock

seven thirty

eight o'clock